Natalia had never felt so helpless. Marc wanted to separate their souls after they had been twin flames forever…

Natalia bolted up from her chair. "Excuse me. I don't know what you're talking about. I don't want to sever my soul from Marc's. This is a huge mistake."

Ophiuchus folded his hands in front of him. "Maybe you don't, my dear, but Marcos does. Do you always believe everything is about you?"

"Yes, sir, she does," Marc answered before she could speak for herself.

"I do not!" Natalia twisted her whole body to face Marc. "What's going on?"

"I'm sorry, but it's time," he said. "You're too difficult and I'm exhausted. I don't think I can go another round with you."

Sometimes the past won't stay where it belongs.

Marc and Natalia are settling into parenthood, but they can't shake the feeling of déjà vu when it comes to their new baby.

Sensing they've been a family before when something horrible happened, they journey back in time, through hypnotic regression, to eighteenth century Belgium, where they relive a shocking past life that challenges their love more than any other and causes repercussions in the present.

Last time, remembering their past lives brought Marc and Natalia together, this time it may tear them apart.

KUDOS for *Forever Flames*

In *Forever Flames* by Debbie Christiana, Marc and Natalia are back. This time Natalia's pregnant and the couple discovers, when the baby is born, that they have issues from a past life with her. Once again, Marc and Nat undergo past-life regression, but now instead of bringing them closer together, it seems to be tearing them apart. …As in the first book in the series, Christiana's characters are almost too realistic. *Forever Flames* is well-written, but much too short for me. As always, Christiana leaves you wanting more. This book is only a novella, so hopefully, a new book in the series will be coming out soon. ~ *Taylor Jones, Reviewer*

Forever Flames by Debbie Christiana is a welcome addition to her *Twin Flames* series…As before, the story is very well written, the characters are believable and charming, and the plot is strong, with some very interesting twists and turns. I was very surprised to see some of the problems that Marc and Nat ran into after their baby was born. Not that the problems weren't realistic, they were. But usually in a series like this, a couple who married in the first book seems to breeze through the second in idyllic bliss, not having a care in the world. Unfortunately, that rarely happens in real life. It's nice to read an author that understands that. ~ *Regan Murphy, Reviewer*

ACKNOWLEDGEMENTS

Thank you to:

Black Opal Books – Lauri, Faith and Joyce, for all your help, support, and edits.

My dear friend and awesome artist, Cindy Hammock, who created the beautiful cover for Forever Flames. Love you!

Jack in the Black Opal Art Department for his finishing touches on the cover.

Terri Lynn DeFino for planting the seed to write the novella.

Nana Prah, Liv Rancourt, Kathy Oliveri and Linda Rose for reading Forever Flames in all its stages and helping me make it a better story.

Linda Rose, medical intern extraordinaire, for answering my rabies questions.

My family, Billy, Matt, Aj, and Ellie – Love you!

Luna, the best Yellow Lab puppy in the world, who sleeps under my desk when I write.

Forever Flames

A Twin Flames Novella

Debbie Christiana

A Black Opal Books Publication

GENRE: PARANORMAL ROMANCE/HISTORICAL ROMANCE

FOREVER FLAMES ~ A Twin Flames Novella
Copyright © 2014 by Debbie Christiana
Cover Design by Cindy Hammock
All cover art copyright © 2014
All Rights Reserved
Print ISBN: 978-1-626941-65-6

First Publication: AUGUST 2014

Published by Black Opal Books **http://www.blackopalbooks.com**

DEDICATION

Nana's Novella.
You know who you are.

Chapter 1

We have a secret in our culture, and it's not that
birth is painful, it's that women are strong.
~ Laura Stavoe Harm

This is all your fault!"
The vise-like grip tightened around Marc's hand.
He held his tongue, as his fingers were on the
verge of breaking. It was hard to believe his beautiful
Natalia, at forty-one, had this much strength in her deli-
cate hand.

They arrived at the hospital in the middle of the
night, happy with the anticipation of bringing their first
child into the world.

Things had changed.

The sun rose and empty coffee cups filled the garbage bin. As the contractions came harder and faster, Natalia's euphoric mood vanished. She had been at this for hours and Marc didn't know where she got the conviction or the stamina.

Whoever coined the phrase "the weaker sex," when referring to women, couldn't have been more wrong. She was propped up in bed with the covers spewed to the side, her cheeks flushed with exhaustion and sweat. Feeling helpless and unsure of what to do, he fed her ice chips and showered her with words of love.

In return, Natalia's tongue had sharpened.

"My fault?" What hadn't been his fault these last few hours, including the lack of world peace and the economic collapse?

"I didn't get in this predicament by myself."

"You should have left me alone then."

She scoffed. "Left *you* alone?"

"Let's face it. You can't keep your hands off me. You have no one to blame but yourself."

"Oh, pleeaazzee." Natalia grimaced. "Get the hell over yourself. This isn't the first time you've gotten me in this mess."

The contraction subsided and she loosened her hold. Marc breathed a sigh of relief that turned into a weary groan. The nurse peered at the two of them over her wire-rimmed glasses, eyebrow cocked and clipboard in hand. "Ms. Santagario, I was under the impression this was your first baby," she said. "Is my information incorrect?"

Natalia didn't answer her. Instead, she gave Marc a haughty expression as her lips curled into a "get-us-out-of-this-jam" smirk.

"Yes, this is our—her—our first baby." Marc tripped over his tongue. "Don't mind her ramblings." He in turn shot Natalia a self-satisfied grin. "She's a crazy bundle of raging female hormones."

The nurse scribbled something on Natalia's chart and headed out the door. "My shift is ending. Your new delivery nurse is Jennifer Herrera. When I see you tomorrow, you'll have a brand new baby. I'll let the doctor know you are in transition."

When they were alone, he leaned over the bed. "You think having our baby is a mess?"

"You aren't the one lying here, are you?"

No, he wasn't and, like most men, he was glad.

Natalia tackled the onset of another contraction and reached for him. Marc made the mistake of hesitation. She had done a job on both of his hands and he needed a minute to decide which one ached less.

As he offered a sacrificial hand, she snapped at him, "If you can't be supportive, then get the hell out of here."

"You're being totally unreasonable." He took a step back. "Were you like this the other times? Because if you were, I'm glad I wasn't there." Marc wrapped her fingers around the metal bar on the side of the bed. "Squeeze this. I'm out of here."

"Good." As the contraction reached its peak, she writhed in pain from side to side, clutching the railings. "I can do it myself," she said, wincing.

Marc stood taut. Could he leave her like this? Even for a short time? He considered himself a patient man. A virtue required in a relationship with Natalia. A fact, he had known for a very, very long time. However, everyone had their limit.

Natalia was right about one thing. She could do it herself. Her strength and passion were two of the many things he loved about her. Neither one meant anything they said just now—it was a stressful circumstance. He'd be back. She'd be glad to see him, and they would be fine. Right now, they needed a break.

Without a word, he slipped out the door, into the hallway of the maternity ward, and waited. He couldn't bring himself to walk away until the new nurse arrived.

A young woman clad in yellow scrubs from head to toe approached him. A hospital hat covered her hair and a paper mask hung around her neck. "Good morning," he said. "Are you our nurse?"

"Yes. It's nice to meet you. I'm Jen."

"I'm Marc. I have to step out for a few minutes and didn't want to leave her alone."

"First time father?"

An odd awareness swept through him. His first reaction was to blurt out a resounding 'no.' Over the course of many millennia and vast amounts of past lives, he had fathered and Natalia had given him many children. What fueled his anxiety was this was the first time he would be part of the incredible experience of bringing his child into the world. All he could manage was a slight nod.

"Don't take too long," Jen warned him. "Transition usually only lasts from 15 minutes to an hour."

"Thanks." He took a step and paused. "Take good care of her. I'll be right back."

"Don't worry, she's in good hands." She pulled open the door and went in.

With one swipe of his hand, the elastic paper cap on his head was off and in the garbage. The gown followed. The signs on the wall directed him to the waiting area. Huddled in the small, cluttered room, a box of donuts between them, were their combined families, patiently waiting for news.

Natalia's brother, Robbie, and his partner of sixteen years, Ben, were deep in conversation over who would win the baby pool the employees of the vineyard had put together.

"If Nat has a boy in the next hour that weighs seven pounds, I win!"

Ben waved the crumbled paper marked with squares

in the air, his charismatic personality and silver-blue eyes shining.

"Don't spend the money so fast, my friend. It's a girl. I've said so from the beginning." Sam, the vineyard's expert wine maker, sat with his arm around Marc's aunt, Mariella. In their sixties and both alone for many years, Marc was glad they had found each other.

Mariella noticed him standing the doorway. "What's wrong, Marcos?" She hurried toward him with her arms open. "You don't look so good. Is Natalia all right?"

Her dark brown eyes flickered with concern. She had raised him from age four when his parent's died, loved Natalia like a daughter and considered this baby her first grandchild.

"She's fine. I just need a little air."

Robbie laughed and slapped his back. "How bad is it in there? Has my sister thrown anything yet or is she just throwing obscenities around?"

"Yeah, she's ready to kill someone. Preferably me," Marc said.

"Maybe we could go in there and face the storm for a few minutes," Sam offered. "We'll need to put on one of those paper gowns."

"You might be better off with a suit of armor," Marc warned. "But do what you want."

The men flagged down a nurse and asked to see the patient in room four-thirty-two.

"Come on, Mariella." Marc put his arm around his aunt. "Let's get a quick cup of coffee. I need to get back."

J J

Natalia rested back against the soft pillow, grateful to have a minute or two before the next contraction. Exhausted, she closed her eyes and let the small pieces of ice linger then melt in her mouth. Such a simple thing gave her so much pleasure.

She'd been hard on Marc, but it made him leave, and that was what she wanted. She loved him and their unborn baby more than anything, but he was getting under her skin. She understood he felt powerless to help her, but shoving spoon after spoon of ice into her mouth, fluffing her pillows, and covering her up after she threw the blankets off, wasn't what she needed. She wanted to be alone.

"Hi, Natalia," the new nurse greeted her. "My name is Jen. I'm your delivery nurse." She flipped through the report from the previous nurse. "Your contractions are coming about three minutes apart?"

So much for time to myself.

"Yes." Natalia caught her breath, wrapped her hands around the sheet and pulled herself through the pain. When the contraction diminished, the nurse checked her

vital signs, guided her feet into the stirrups and positioned herself at the foot of the bed. The amount of traf-
fic between her legs since she'd arrived did wonders for
her modesty.

"Good news. You're almost at ten centimeters. I'm
going to call Dr. Kapoor."

The nurse left and Natalia relished some time alone
when she heard a voice.

"Hey, sis." Robbie poked his head around the open
door. "Is it safe to come in? I picked the short straw and
they sent me in to assess the situation."

"Very funny." The three men shuffled in wearing
their paper gowns. A small giggle escaped her. "You
look like the Three Stooges."

"You're doing fine aren't you, doll?" asked Ben.

An intense tightness ran across her belly. Natalia
grabbed the bed rail. "Holy fucking shit!"

Robbie flew to the bedside and cradled her head.
"Nat, sweetie, the expression is 'a mouth like a sailor.'
Well, we're the sailors. How about you leave the swear-
ing to us?"

"Did you come to help me or give me a hard time?"
she snapped.

"Rob, leave her be. No one else is here." Ben
reached over and wiped her sweat soaked hair away from
her face.

"Thanks, Ben." Robbie's lover of sixteen years was

like a brother to her. Natalia motioned to the older man she loved like a father. "Hi, Sam. Come here, I won't bite, contrary to what Marc has probably told you."

Another contraction struck and Natalia grabbed his hand. Her powerful grip caused him to yelp. "Whoa, Nat. If you want me to continue to make wine, I need my fingers." Sam opened and closed his fist then shook his hand.

Dr. Kapoor, an attractive Indian woman of slight build and an abundance of energy, burst through the door. "Natalia, how's my favorite patient doing?"

She massaged her belly. "I'd be fine if it weren't for these damn contractions harassing me every few seconds."

"No contractions, no baby. Your wonderful body works that way. It knows what to do and won't give you more than you can handle. The last few centimeters are the hardest." Dr. Kapoor settled herself at the end of the bed and guided Natalia's feet back into the stirrups. "It won't be long before it's time to push."

In single file the three men kissed Natalia good-bye. "We love you, sis," said Robbie as they walked out the door.

With her mouth open to answer, an intense contraction took her breath. She reached for the bed railing, but a strong hand clenched hers. She didn't have to look to know it was Marc.

When the contraction was over, he cupped her face in his hands and kissed her. "I love you."

"I love you, too."

"Okay, Natalia, it's show time," announced Dr. Kapoor.

♨ ♨

Giovanna's warm, safe world closed in on her. Tighter and tighter, it squeezed. The worst part of life on earth was getting there. People didn't want to die. Dying was easy compared to this.

With each shove, her head bumped against a hard surface and she ended up back where she started. Frustrated that she had no control over what was happening to her, all she could do was suffer through the jostling around. She knew what was ahead. The thrusts would come faster and harder and her temporary living space would narrow. She would briefly lose her awareness and without realizing what was happening, she'd be propelled into a completely new world.

♨ ♨

"Come on, Natalia. One more good push and you'll be able to hold your precious baby." With Dr. Kapoor's calm nature and encouraging but firm directions, Natalia had visions of an easy childbirth. She was in a hospital with modern medical advancements that hadn't been available to her in the frigid hut of prehistoric times, the Middle Ages, or the lodge of the Omaha Indians, when she'd given birth in her previous lives.

She handled the pain well until the last few hours and then it was too late for drugs. They told her the baby, too, would feel the effects. So once again, she was in this time-honored position, pushing after hours of labor and contractions.

"I know what to do. I'm too tired. I don't think I can." Her tongue and lips so dry, she was surprised to hear her own words.

"Nat, you can do it." Marc's whisper tickled against her ear. "You can't give up now, baby. Do it for G."

At Marc's mention of Giovanna, or G, his nickname for her, tears burned Natalia's eyes. Not tears of pain but of love for the presence that had lived with her for so long, the determined but playful apparition she and Marc had come to love. When Natalia was six months pregnant, G disappeared. Mariella's theory was that G was someone from their past, and she wouldn't be surprised if when they looked deep into their new baby's eyes, it would be Giovanna staring back at them.

Natalia managed a smile amid her exhaustion. "If it's G, she's being her normal stubborn self."

"It's her. I'm sure of it." This time he squeezed her

hand. "Come on, baby, let's meet Giovanna. I've missed her as much as you have."

Natalia's body ached for sleep but the overwhelming urge to push would soon come. Her tired and stiff fingers of her free hand gripped the handles on one side of the bed.

"Don't stop now, Natalia," Dr. Kapoor encouraged her. "You're almost there."

She mustered up the little strength she had left and pulled herself up to a semi-seated position. With a loud groan, she pushed with all she had. The next few minutes were a distorted blur, until she heard the baby cry.

"It's a girl!" Marc yelled. "Baby, you did it. She's beautiful."

Chapter 2

Only those who have dared to let go
can dare to re-enter.
~ *Meister Eckhart*

Every horrible sensation hit Giovanna at once. She was taken from her warm surroundings with an abrupt yank. A chill prickled her skin. Her calm, dark atmosphere with the soothing heartbeat was gone, replaced by loud clamoring sounds and blinding light.

She disliked the confinement to her new, heavy, and burdensome body, which she would have to learn to maneuver once again. She preferred the light, free feeling of her true nature.

People naturally attached themselves to their bodies. Eventually, she would too.

She dreaded this part of re-entering humanity. She was uncomfortable and unhappy and did the only thing she could.

She let out a piercing wail.

The more hands that grabbed at her the louder she screamed.

Then a burst of warmth engulfed her as she was placed down. She heard a soft rhythmic beat in her ear. It was faint but familiar and comforting. Her cries slowed then stopped.

There were voices. She knew them well. They spoke of love to her every day.

Her eyes popped open but her new world was fuzzy and unclear. She couldn't make out their faces but she was where she belonged.

She eased into the tranquil pulse of the heartbeat and the gentle stroking on her back.

The long, rough journey was over. Everything she had to do to get here was worth it.

All that mattered was they were together.

♨ ♨

"Natalia, meet your little girl." Jen placed the baby on Natalia's belly. "Skin to skin contact between mother and baby is important in the first few minutes of life. I'll clean her up then cover her."

Marc wiped his eyes with the back of his hand. "Have you ever seen such a gorgeous baby girl?"

Natalia didn't think she could love something so much.

"Look what we did, at what we made. She's perfect." Natalia couldn't take her eyes off the little person she and Marc had created. "She has black curls like you." She laughed between sniffles. "I can't believe it. I thought my time had passed to have a baby and here she is." With her free hand, Natalia grabbed Marc's. "Thank you so much."

"Baby, don't thank me. Whatever we do, we do together."

"Natalia," Dr. Kapoor said, "you only need a few stitches. This shouldn't take too long. Just relax and enjoy your baby."

Natalia felt a few tugs and pulls, but the happiness in her heart pushed away any uncomfortable sensation between her legs. She didn't know if was a natural instinct or memories of the past, but with Marc's help, she inched herself higher against the pillows and cradled the baby in her left arm, offering her left breast.

Jen came toward the bed. "Okay, should we try nursing? I can help you if you need—" The nurse, with an expression of utter confusion on her face, paused. "Oh, I see you've already gotten the hang of it."

"It's really quite easy if you just relax and do what nature intended," Natalia remarked.

"First time mothers aren't always as calm as you. That comes with second or third births." Jen eased a pillow under Natalia's arm that supported the baby. "If you need anything let me know. Would you like me to dim the lights? I can put music on too, if you'd like."

"That would be great, thanks," Marc said.

He released the side railing of the bed and snuggled in with Natalia and the baby. He put his arm around her and she laid her head against him.

"She's amazing, isn't she?" He then shifted his head as if he were going to speak to the pillow but whispered in her ear. "What do think, Nat? Is it G?"

"You're all set, Natalia." Dr. Kapoor stood on the other side of the bed. "You three make a beautiful family." She squeezed Natalia's arm. "You did great. I know you've wanted this for a long time. We'll leave you to bond and then come back."

"Thank you for everything," Natalia said.

When she was gone, Natalia said, "I feel a connection, don't you?"

"Yes," Marc said, "but she's our little girl, its normal. I think we need to look into her eyes."

"She's fallen asleep."

Natalia no sooner spoke than the baby flailed her

arms and legs, thrashing free from underneath the blanket.

Her eyes flew open and locked with theirs.

"Oh my God," they gasped in unison.

Natalia was in an elated daze. This was different from the instant attraction and magnetism of when she first saw Marc. It was a powerful emotion all its own. As if a chemical reaction had surged fusing them together. "Marc, do you feel it? It's really her."

Marc's jaw hung wide open. "Yes, baby, I feel it." He moved in closer, putting his other arm around the front of Natalia, and held them tight against him. When he released them, their baby was back asleep.

"Giovanna," Natalia said. "We love you so much."

Marc kissed the top of her small head. "Oh, G, sweetie, what are we going to call you?"

"I only know her as Giovanna." Natalia shrugged. "What's wrong with that?"

"It's too long. That's why I called her G to begin with. Unless," he paused, "we call her Gigi, for the first two letters of Giovanna." He gave Natalia a guarded gaze from the corner of his eye. "What do you think?"

"I think you're handsome, sexy, and a genius. Gigi Tremonti, I love it! It sounds very exotic." She lifted her head and kissed him. "And I know you're going to be a great father."

Chapter 3

We all have some experience of a feeling that comes
over us occasionally, of what we are saying and doing
have been said and done before, in a remote time
– of our having been surrounded, dim ages ago
by the same faces, objects and circumstances.
~ *Charles Dickens* (David Copperfield)

The two people Marc loved more than anything
flooded his thoughts. Picturing a naked Natalia
in the shower with water pouring over her body
made him want to burst in and take her by surprise. It
was maddening to be so close to her and not have her.
But it was too soon. She'd let him know when she was
ready. Until then, he'd continue to chop wood to rid him-

self of his frustration. At this rate, they'd have a surplus for winters to come.

He glanced down at Gigi, lying on her back in the middle of the king sized bed, her lips moving in a small sucking motion. It was hard to fathom that his precious little girl and their beloved ghost, Giovanna, were together in one perfect package. When Nat asked him to watch her he was sure she didn't mean sit like a sentinel guarding a treasure, but he couldn't take his eyes off his baby girl.

He stroked her dark hair and the same thought that had haunted his mind since she was born resurfaced. "Gigi, sweetie, who are you?"

Many scenarios ran through his head. Was she a past sister, child, or close friend? Had something gone wrong between them? Or were they separated by death before they had finished their purpose? He carefully scooped her up in his arms, supporting her delicate head. He walked across the room and, without warning, froze in front of the window.

He was suddenly agitated, at what, he didn't know. A grim voice whispered deep inside his brain of things he couldn't make out and wasn't sure he wanted to hear. Still, it dangled and teased him.

He closed his eyes and concentrated. He—almost—had it.

Then it was gone.

Marc's eyes flew open. He held his breath, tense as a board from his neck to his feet.

He exhaled and relaxed slowly, so as not to disturb his little girl asleep in his arms.

As he recovered from his powerful moment of déjà vu he looked at Gigi. "What secrets are you keeping?"

♨ ♨

"Did she get you?" Natalia joked.

"Yep. I had her on my shoulder and up came her last meal, all over me. I guess I jiggled her too much." Marc had his bare back to her, rummaging through the drawer, looking for a clean shirt.

"Babies strike without warning." Natalia moved behind him and placed her hands on his back. "Wait a minute before you put your shirt on."

Marc's head bolted straight up. She knew what he wanted, but could only offer a different type of intimacy right now.

The tip of her finger went to his left shoulder where his birthmark told their remarkable love story. The physical scars from past lives they'd shared had always reappeared on his body. Marks scared on his skin from protecting her or their love over the millennia. Snake bites, burns, arrow wounds, and small pox blemishes were things he'd endured for her. Before they met, and without understanding why, he had two entwined flames tattooed around his birthmark.

It brought them together the first night they'd met and bonded them forever.

As was her habit, she rose on her tiptoes and kissed his shoulder. A soft groan escaped Marc as she wrapped her arms around his waist.

"Hey, baby," he said and held her arms tightly around him.

It might not be the display of affection he'd hoped for, but she knew that one small act would bring them together in a divine closeness only they shared.

"I love you," she said. "We've been busy with Gigi and our future, but I don't want to ever forget our past."

"I know, baby. I love you, too." He undid her arms and turned to face her. "Speaking of the past, there's something I'd like to ask you."

"Sure." She let the damp towel fall off her head. Brush in hand, she checked Gigi, snoozing on the bed, and began to untangle her own wet hair.

"Do you ever wonder about our other time or times with Gigi?"

Natalia stopped mid-stroke. Apprehension clogged her throat. "What?"

"Aren't you curious as to why she worked so hard to get us together?"

"Because we're Twin Flame soul mates and are supposed to be together." She tackled the knot in her hair, hoping this conversation would be a short one.

"Yeah, but then she was reborn as our daughter just as Mariella predicted."

"I love Mariella and I know she's the expert on reincarnation, but it may have been a lucky guess."

"Do you really believe that?"

No. "Maybe she wanted to be raised by fabulous parents." Natalia planted a fake smile on her face.

"Something weird happened while you were in the shower." Marc eased the brush from her fingers and turned her head so he had her full attention. "I had a déjà vu moment and not a good one. I can't say for sure it was about Gigi, but I was holding her while thinking about our past."

"Maybe we were family before. Families are reborn together all the time—they just don't know it. We're different. We do know it and it's hard to adjust to." She headed toward the bathroom.

"No. Something bad happened and I think I was responsible." He hesitated. "I want you and I to be regressed."

She grabbed the back of her calf and cried out in pain. The feeling of burning embers pressed against her skin brought her to her knees.

It lasted only seconds and she reached for the doorframe for balance.

"Nat, you okay?" Marc caught her as she went down. "You're pale as a ghost."

"I'm—okay." *Then why does it feel like a freight train is rattling through my gut?* "Stupid leg cramp. That's all."

He got her back on her feet. "Will you at least consider being regressed?" She stared at him, no words coming from her dry throat. "Nat?"

"No." She took two steps toward him and leaned her body against his, her arms dangling at her sides. "It's not you, it's me."

"What?"

As his strong arms pulled her into his chest, she questioned her reluctance to tell him. He'd seen her at her worst and still loved her. "When Gigi was still Giovanna the apparition, she came to me and lived here. She didn't go to you." She licked her lips, which were as dry as her mouth. "There's a dark cloud of guilt that hangs over me when I think of who Gigi could have been to us. It's me. I did something awful." She clicked her tongue. "I don't know why I'm so thirsty. You don't have a water bottle, do you?"

"Baby, I can't imagine you doing something awful." He pushed her wet hair from her face. "Anyway, G loved you when she was here with you."

"Water, please?"

"Oh, sure, over here on the night stand."

Marc went for the drink and Natalia sat back down on the bed near Gigi. "I know she did and I loved her. The only thing that helps me when I get that dreadful feeling is knowing she has forgiven me."

He handed her a small, half-filled water bottle. "Sorry, that's all that's left."

She chugged it down in four gulps. "Thanks." She touched the side of his face and gave him a tender kiss. "I don't want you to worry about anything. You did nothing wrong. She adores you as much as you adore her. It's my burden and I can deal with it."

"I don't buy it." He got up and paced back and forth, his hand rubbing the back of his neck. "That doesn't explain my bad feeling, and she showed herself to me, too. Whatever went down, we're in it together. The best thing to do is find out. You know you don't do well with guilt." He reached down and stroked her hand. "You're still not over the one night we—"

She pulled away from him. "Don't!"

"See what I mean?"

"I don't want to know what happened. I want to start fresh. I promised her I'd do everything right this time." The roof of her mouth was like sandpaper. She scanned the room for another water bottle.

"How can we do it right if we don't know what we did wrong? Baby, please, just think about it. That's all I'm asking."

"I'm not up to it right now. Gigi is only two weeks old. I need more time."

"I know."

His big brown eyes were so hopeful, she found him hard to resist. Maybe he was right. Their last regression helped clear up many unexplained issues.

It still scared the shit out of her.

Her parched throat constricted. "Okay. I'll think about it."

His face brightened like a child getting a much-anticipated gift. "I'll call Mariella. It'll take a few weeks to set up—in case you agree. Something tells me it's the right thing to do."

With a quick peck to her lips, he bolted out the door and down the steps. Natalia ran into the bathroom and turned the cold faucet on, scooping handfuls of water into her mouth as fast as she could. When that didn't help, she lowered her head underneath the cool stream and opened her mouth.

Nothing would quench her thirst.

♨ ♨

Natalia and Gigi were in her office, curled up in a leather recliner near the window. The mid-March sun shone through the glass basking them in the perfect temperature of warmth.

Gigi sucked happily at Natalia's breast.

"You're too damn cute. You know, I can't decide if my insatiable thirst and burning leg—yes, I lied to Daddy—are signs we should be regressed or warning us against it. What do you think?"

Gigi's answer was a tiny yawn. Natalia draped a small towel over shoulder, lifted Gigi against her and patted her back. "Just as I expected. Pleading the fifth, huh?"

Burp!

"Good girl. Ready for the other side?"

She offered her baby her other breast but Gigi wouldn't latch on. Instead, her wide eyes held Natalia in a hypnotic stare.

A familiar sensation fluttered at the base of her neck. It was the same feeling she would get when Giovanna the apparition communicated telepathically with her.

Natalia waited with nervous patience for the subconscious message but nothing came.

"Gigi, you can do it, sweet pea. Tell me what to do. Do you want us to know what happened so long ago?"

The baby startled in Natalia's arms as a sudden burst of loving and peaceful energy rippled through her. But it wasn't the answer she expected.

Gigi was happy.

She understood and accepted why things happened the way they had.

The regression would be for their benefit, for them to forgive themselves. With the full impact of what her little one had told her, Natalia sat in awe.

Gigi was fast asleep.

"Oh, you poor thing, you must be exhausted. You're a special little girl and we love you."

She nestled Gigi into her neck and gave her a gentle hug while an ominous question picked at her brain.

What the hell had they done?

Chapter 4

You're a fire in my soul that can never by extinguished.
~ Unknown

Natalia's naked reflection glared back at her. The twelve-year age difference between her and Marc hadn't plagued her thoughts. But as she stood exposed in front of a mirror, that had no intention of lying to her, it crossed her mind. Her gaze fixed itself on her stomach and the two long purple lines that ran across the lower part of her abdomen. She'd rubbed the damn aloe vera and lavender oil on her expanding belly every day of her pregnancy, three times a day, and it still looked like a goddamn road map tattooed on her skin.

With her hands on her hips, she twisted first to the

left, then right, stretching to get a glimpse behind her. On the whole, the package wasn't too bad. Gigi hadn't impacted her ass and long legs, for which she was grateful. She had six more baby pounds to lose. Owning and working at a vineyard was a physical job and with her daily walks through the acres of grape vines, she was confident she could shed those pesky pounds by early summer.

She gazed upward at her boobs. Full and round, in part thanks to Gigi and in part to nature. She had been bestowed with what a high school friend of her brother's had once referred to as "a nice rack." Robbie immediately punched him in the mouth. The "girls" might not be in the exact spot they were a decade ago, but they held their own.

One last sweep over her entire self and Natalia decided to stop worrying about body image. Her love of good Italian food and wine was who she was. She wouldn't change that, even for a few pounds. And Marc wouldn't want her to. The chef in him loved to cook for her and appreciated her appetite. He was food. She was wine.

As in so many other ways, they complimented each other perfectly.

The gurgle of water spilling into the Jacuzzi reminded her of why she came into the bathroom in the first place.

Tomorrow was their regression.

She was ready, but a foreboding finger still tapped her on the shoulder, making her wonder what she had done that frightened her so much.

Ordering the unpleasant thoughts away, Natalia lit vanilla-and-sandalwood-scented candles and placed them on the wooden lip around the Jacuzzi. With a press of a button, Ray LaMontagne's sultry voice flowed from her iHome asking some lucky woman if he could stay with her tonight. She left the door ajar and dimmed the lights.

The tub was almost full and with a quick turn to the left, the hot water knob stopped its noisy flow. She dipped one foot in ankle deep and swirled the water around in a small circle. Perfect. As her entire body melted into the soothing warmth, she leaned her head back against the wall of the tub and sank deeper into the water. Gigi was fed and asleep, Natalia hoped, for more than four hours. She reached for the bottle of 2007 Santagario Merlot—their favorite—poured two glasses, and let Ray's serenade do the rest.

"Are you expecting someone?"

Marc's heart pounded in his chest. Natalia's thick black hair was pulled up on top of her head, her long swan neck glistening with beads of water. As the generous curves of her breasts peeked out from the surface of the water, his arousal grew.

In a graceful motion, she raised her wine glass to him. "Yes, I am. I think you better leave before he gets here."

She took a slow, deliberate sip of her wine and swept her pink tongue across her lips.

Marc felt like a teenager on his first date. His sexy, flirtatious Natalia was back.

He knew she'd return to him, but shit, he'd missed her. He knew the exact number of days, hours, minutes, and seconds that had passed since the last time he had her.

The end of her pregnancy and recovery had intruded on their sex life.

He'd expected it, understood it, and was patient but, lately, everything she did gave him a hard on. Earlier, when she'd bent over to put logs on the fire, he stifled a groan, left the room, and went outside for a brisk walk. He'd always been a pushover for her sweet ass.

He was hard as a rock and shifted in discomfort. "I got here first. His loss."

"Maybe we should give him another minute." Natalia casually lifted her leg and swung it up over the edge. "If he isn't here by then—" She gave him a shameless glance from head to toe. "—you'll do nicely."

She arched back with ease, nipples erect, and legs

parted in an erotic invitation he longed for. Her dark eyes smoldered with desire.

Lust shimmered through him. "Time's up."

♨ ♨

Natalia bit her lip in anticipation as Marc pulled off his shirt. It was moments like this that she appreciated his youth. She loved his body but since he'd left his job as a chef, his physique had become more toned and defined; thanks to chopping wood, lugging cases of wine, and moving fifty-gallon wine barrels.

Men were certainly experts at getting their clothes off in record time when the need arose and Marc was no exception. A quick click from his belt and his jeans joined the rest of his clothes on the floor.

He lifted the second glass of wine into the air. "Luckily, your friend and I like the same wine."

"Mmm?"

She hadn't heard a word he'd said. Her eyes travelled across his broad chest, down his lean stomach leading to his slender hips, which she had an uncontrollable urge to wrap her legs around as tight as she could. Not to mention his...um...had she really gone this long without him? She mentally counted the weeks on her fingers. What the hell was wrong with her? The answer was simple—exhaustion. At the end of the day, she looked forward to time with Marc but when she climbed into bed and her head hit the pillow, sleep overcame her. Tonight would prove different. "Marc, you need to get in the tub." She gulped. "Now."

The side of his mouth twisted in a smirk. "I thought you—"

"Get in the damn tub."

♨ ♨

Marc focused on Natalia as her foot slinked up his chest and rested on his shoulder. With a tender hand he massaged her ankle then traced the soft, smooth curve of her calf with his finger. He paused behind her knee, circling the delicate spot with his thumb. Natalia put down her wine glass, braced her hands against the side of the tub, and sat up.

Her face was flushed with desire as he held out his hand to her.

She was on him like metal to a magnet. Waves of water crashed around them. Her hands glided up the sides of his head and her fingers tangled in his hair.

Pulling his head back, she kissed him like a crazed woman.

She climbed farther on top of him and he sunk deeper into water.

"Whoa, Nat." His arms flopped in the water trying to

get his balance but all he accomplished was a lot of splashing. "I'm—"

"Very sexy," Natalia purred.

"Well." He chuckled. "Thanks, but you're—"

"Horny as hell. I can't believe we haven't done this sooner."

Her lips crashed down on his again, her tongue rolling around in his mouth. He was up to his neck in water and sinking fast. He tried to grip the wet sides of the tub but his hands slipped away.

Leave it to Natalia to almost drown him with passion. When his time came, he'd be happy to go, having his hot-blooded, voluptuous Natalia all over him. God, he loved her and her *enthusiasm,* but it wasn't his time to leave this world yet.

"Nat, baby." He grabbed her hips and lifted her straight up like he was bench-pressing her body. "I want you, too. More than anything," he gasped. "But I need to breathe."

He eased her down in the water and she laughed. "I'm sorry." She floated toward him and cupped his face. "You looked so handsome. I've missed *us.*"

This time her lips caressed his with gentle affection.

He locked his arms around her waist. "Me, too. But we're together now."

♨ ♨

Sweeping Natalia from the tub, Marc wrapped her in a towel and eased her into a chair. Ray's crooning and the soft glow from the candles had followed them into their bedroom, creating a seductive atmosphere. Natalia's left leg was now slung over the arm of the chair instead of the lip of the tub. Inch by inch he dried her entire body, his warm mouth trailing behind the towel, beginning with her neck, to her breasts, stopping only to let his tongue drive her to distraction before he leisurely nibbled down her belly.

The towel slid off her leg onto the floor. He pressed his hand against her knee, opening her farther for him. As Marc's hot mouth teased her inner thigh, his fingers played with her sex, now burning with agonizing desire.

"Sweet mother of Jesus, Marc," she rasped. "Please."

"Patience, baby, patience."

When she couldn't take his torture any longer, his mouth rolled over the crossway between her legs. A yelp of delight escaped her with every delectable flick of his tongue. Natalia tensed. She sat up and leaned toward him, grabbing the back of his head. Her body twitched as ripples of pleasure spiraled upward from deep in her core. She tugged his hair and arched her back in one final climactic spasm.

"I see you haven't lost your touch," she gasped and fell back in the cushioned chair.

♨ ♨

Marc didn't let her catch her breath. He popped her on her feet, imprisoned in his arms. Their bodies blended, skin against skin. His erection jutted against her. He gave her ass a love swat then grabbed her tone, round globes. "It's been too long, baby."

"Words are overrated."

Natalia pushed him flat on his back on the bed. Like a wildcat on a hunt, she slinked on all fours toward him. An expert at the art of seduction, he never wanted a woman as much as he did her.

She leaned over him and traced his lips with the tip of her tongue. She nibbled at his neck, down his chest, circling his belly button, as her hand strayed between his legs.

She said she loved him but what she was doing was about to kill him.

"You know," he moaned, "I've pretty much had a hard on for you since before Gigi was born. You're gonna have to help me out here and quick." After what he'd seen in the delivery room, if he were a woman, he'd keep his legs crossed, so nothing like that ever happened again. "We'll go easy if—"

Natalia's head popped up from her wanton grazing south of his lower abdomen. Her jet-black locks framed her salacious smile. "Easy?"

"Sure…if you're…um…I don't know." He sighed. "Could you go back to what you were doing?"

No. Instead, she turned her back to him and hoisted her right leg over him like she was hopping on a motorcycle. *Is she really doing this*? He could only hope. He bent his legs. She placed one hand on his knee for balance, grabbed his hardness with the other and slid him with ease inside her wetness. This was one of his favorite ways to make love. Seeing her lovely ass move up and down while watching himself glide in and out of her was a massive turn on for him and she knew it.

She held both his knees, rocking her hips in a circular motion once or twice before riding him hard and fast, clenching him with searing pleasure. Their bodies reunited in a ravenous frenzy of need, lust, and passion. The recent absence of their sexual encounters affected his self-control.

"Come on, Nat!" he shouted. "I can't hold out much longer."

Natalia's nails dug into his knees and her cries of passion filled the room.

After weeks of longing for Natalia's supple body, Marc spiraled toward release. He shuddered as he called her name, his body surrendering everything he had to her.

〰 〰

Natalia fell back against Marc. His right arm lay across her chest cupping her left breast, his other arm wrapped tight around her waist.

"You're amazing," he murmured, tickling her neck with his warm lips. "I love all the ways you do me, but that was especially sweet."

Natalia cherished the time following their lovemaking. She sank deep into his tender embrace. Sometimes Marc would drift off to sleep while still entwined with her, but she didn't mind. The rhythm of his peaceful breathing soothed her, leaving her happy that he was content.

Tonight was different.

Marc's hands playfully caressed and fondled her. She hoped he wasn't done with her.

He broke their blissful silence. "Are you thinking about tomorrow?"

"Yeah, a little. Are you?" Natalia shifted loose from his arms and stretched out long beside him.

Marc stroked the curve of her hip with his thumb. "I'm thinking about you. This time will be different. We both know that. I want you to be sure."

"I told you what happened with Gigi. Whether I'm sure or not, we need to do it."

"We agree something bad happened. I still think it was me, but if it becomes too much for you, promise me you'll stop the regression."

"No." She cupped his face and kissed him. "If we start it, we finish it. It's the only way."

Marc rolled on his back and folded his arm over his eyes. "I know you're doing this for me and I love you for it. How about I'll keep the regression going but you stop. That way we'll get the answers we need and save you from–"

She pressed a finger to his lips to quiet him. "No, we're in this together." She rested her head on his chest. "I think we could make better use of our alone time, don't you? You know I would do anything for you. End of discussion."

In one swift movement, Marc flipped her on her back and shackled her arms above her head. "I'm glad to hear that." He moved on top of her. "Because there's something I need you to do for me right now."

She wound her legs tightly around him and thrust her pelvis upward. "My pleasure."

Chapter 5

The past is never where you think you left it.
~ Katharine Anne Porter,
American Novelist 1890-1980

N atalia, you seem restless. It'll be difficult if not impossible to regress you if you're anxious. Did you hurt your leg?"

It was at Dr. Ellis's question that Natalia realized she was kneading the back of her calf. "No, just a cramp." She stood and gave her leg a couple of good shakes. "Let me try to walk it off."

She strolled around her vineyard office, usually a place of solace for her, but today she felt like an inmate on death row, her own home a prison cell.

"Can I get you some water?"

"No thank you." Natalia poured herself a glass of water from the ice-filled pitcher she was compelled to bring to her regression. After a few loud slugs the glass was empty. She refilled it. "I've been so thirsty today."

"Are you worried about leaving Gigi with Robbie and Ben?"

"No. Her uncles will take good care of her."

"She's beautiful. I got to peek at her before I came here to see you."

"Yes, she is." Thinking of her daughter gave Natalia a fleeting moment of comfort. "We're very fortunate she chose us to be her parents."

"She most likely feels she's the lucky one."

Dr. Ellis flashed her perfect white-toothed smile. Natalia studied the woman who had become her friend since her and Marc's last regression. They were similar in age. The doctor's black-rimmed glasses were pushed up on her head and she sat, like the attractive professional she was, in her blue business suit with her legs crossed.

"I'm not so sure about that," Natalia mumbled.

"Is that why I'm here today? To help you find out about your past with Gigi?"

Natalia gave her a solemn nod.

Dr. Ellis walked toward her and rested a reassuring hand on her shoulder. "I forgot the power cord for my computer. Let me go grab it and give you a few minutes to decide if this is what you want to do."

"It's that obvious?"

"Maybe a little," she said. "Take your time." Dr. Ellis's heels clicked on the hardwood floor and the door shut with a soft thud.

Natalia remained in the middle of the small room. For so long the decor had reflected her personality alone, now it was sprinkled with pieces of Marc and Gigi. On the wall next to the vineyard's awards hung Marc's diploma from the Culinary Institute of America. A stuffed teddy bear rested in Gigi's basinet, which stood in front of the bay window.

She didn't want to do this alone and needed Marc with her. But that was impossible. He was upstairs in the guest room with Dr. Collier, getting ready for his own journey back in time. Dread pressed hard against her soul. The long past she and Marc shared wasn't always easy.

At times, it was difficult and cruel, but she had relived all of it without the sense of alarm she felt now.

Marc's white chef's jacket lay draped over the back of the leather recliner in the corner. She stroked her fingers over his embroidered name and remembered how handsome he looked in the fitted coat the night they met. She slipped it on.

His faint scent mixed with garlic and onions still lingered from the last time he had worn it. His closeness wrapped her in a cloak of protection and love. She picked up the stuffed bear from the bassinet and held it tight. Her resolve slowly returned. This was what Marc wanted and what Gigi told her would ease her mind.

There was a light tapping on the door. Natalia buttoned the oversized jacket and pushed up the long sleeves. She nestled deep in her leather recliner with the plush animal secure on her lap. Thinking she looked ridiculous but not caring she called to Dr. Ellis, "Come in, I'm ready."

♨ ♨

"Hey, Doc." Marc kissed Dr. Collier on her cheek. "It's been a long time."

He had known her for as long as he could remember. She was Mariella's dear friend and one of the most qualified therapists he'd known. A woman, with salt and pepper hair, she approached her profession with competency and humor.

Dr. Collier returned his kiss. "We miss you being in the city and stopping in to visit us."

"Thank you for doing the regression here. With Gigi so little, it would have been hard to be away for so long." He showed her to her seat. "Is this all right?"

"We only need two seats and a place to set up my

computer so we can video your regression." She relaxed in her chair and unpacked her computer from its soft bag resting on her knees. "So why am I here today?"

He leaned forward in his chair and rubbed his hands together like he was warming them over a roaring fire. "You know about Giovanna and Gigi, right?"

"Yes. Mariella said you gave her permission to tell me and Dr. Ellis." She zipped her bag shut and laid it on the floor. "Between apparitions, birthmarks, and being soul mates for thousands of years, you two certainly lead interesting lives, don't you?" She booted up the laptop and peered over the screen at him with a look of admiration. "I'm almost jealous."

"Being with Nat has been a wild trip through time for sure. But I think there is one more life we should revisit. I know Gigi got us together so we could be her parents, but I'd like to know why. Nat and I believe something terrible happened."

"I see. Sometimes it's wiser to learn your lessons with no memory of the past, to make the decisions you must without knowing the circumstances behind them," Dr. Collier said. "How does Natalia feel about it?"

"She was apprehensive at first, but it's what we both want."

"Good." Dr. Collier positioned her computer on the table to face Marc. "Since we're not at the center in New

York, we'll have to improvise with the recording of your session."

Marc made a loopy face at the camera. "Hey, Nat. See you in the past or on the other side or wherever the hell we're going." He put his fingers to his lips then pressed them against the screen. "Love you."

"Let's begin." Dr. Collier retrieved a pad and pen from her bag. "We're going to go back the same way we did last time. I'm required to tell you that you will be awake and in control the whole time. The only thing I'm doing is taking you deep into your subconscious. Close your eyes and take deep breathes. Find a place of peace and safety. A place where your body is relaxed, your mind tranquil, but also aware."

Marc leaned back in his chair and surrendered to his friend's soothing words. Between his trust for her and his longing for answers, it was easy to let go.

"Find your hallway and nod your head when you get there."

Marc was bound in blackness. Soon a long hall came into focus. Doors of various colors and materials lined each side. He signaled to Dr. Collier.

"Do you see the door you are looking for?"

Instead of him moving down the corridor, the walls progressed past him.

One by one the doors swept by and then, he saw it. It was at the end on the left side.

"Yes."

"Can you describe it?"

"It glass. Colorful, but fragile."

"Do you want to open it?"

"Yes."

"When you open the door, where are you?"

Marc remained silent, appreciating the recollections filling his mind. "In bed. Eline is moving beneath me as only she can. Her legs are tucked around mine. Her hands are at the small of my back—"

"Marc."

"Pressing me into her."

"Marc!"

"Yes?"

"You know I enjoy you and Natalia's regressions. They are so lively compared to the others we do, but we've been through this before. Remember? Any intimate memories you have are wonderful but best kept to yourself. Got it?"

"Sorry."

"Let's try again and I'll rephrase the question to be on the safe side." She chuckled. "What is the year and country? What is your name and who is Eline?"

"I'm Maarten Vandenberghe. Eline is my wife and we live in Belgium. The year is seventeen-thirty-eight."

"Is Eline someone to you in your present life?"

"Natalia."

"So, unlike the other times, this life isn't about how you two met?"

"No, this is about me, Eline, and our fifteen year old daughter, Alijse."

"Do you recognize Alijse as someone in this life?"

"Yes. Gigi."

"Marc, you may begin when you're ready at the place where it's the most helpful for you to get the answers you need."

Chapter 6

Death is not the greatest evil.
It is worse to want to die and not be able to.
~ Sophtiocles, Greek Playwright 496-406 BC

Five, four, three, two…one. Natalia you should be in a deep relaxed state." Dr. Ellis's voice was comforting and calm.

"Yes."

"Go deeper inside yourself and find that place of infinite knowledge and peace to receive what you need from the door you open."

A twisted and gnarled wooden door appeared, calling to her.

Natalia stiffened.

"Are you all right?"

Natalia licked her lips and her hand fumbled on top of the table for her water.

"Does this door frighten you?"

"Yes."

"Should we look for another door?" Dr. Ellis asked.

"No, this is the one I need."

"Are you sure?"

"Yes."

"Very well. Begin when you're ready."

"I'm Eline Vandenberghe, wife of Maarten, and mother of two grown boys and one girl, Alijse."

"Do you recognize them from other lives you've had?"

"Maarten is Marc. He's a glass blower and expert stain-glass maker. He does most of his work for St. Hubert's Basilica here in the Belgian Ardennes. My sons have been with us before, but it's Alijse that is with us this time. She's Gigi."

"Was it difficult for you and Maarten to be together like it was in some other lives?"

"No. Our families knew each other and we fell in love at first sight. He was born with strange marks on his left shoulder. In my heart I believe they somehow make him mine. Every night I kiss his shoulder before bed."

Natalia pulled the soft bear close to her heart. "Our life has been good. It's the end that's grim."

♨ ♨

MARC...

"I hear Eline yelling in the woods near her garden. I don't give it much thought. A stray dog had found its way in to her and Alijse's heart a year ago. He comes and goes but has wandered off for sometime. Eline has gone up to call for him. But now the shouting is louder. There is fear in her screams. I grab my cloak and run outside.

"Eline is backed up against the split-rail fence of her garden. She's stomping her feet and brandishing a large dead branch in front of her. The animal's movements are jerky. It's staggering aimlessly and a belligerent snarl vibrates from deep in its throat. Long drips of spittle hang like icicles from its mouth. The dog has gone mad.

"I fear my heart will punch through my chest, it's beating so hard. Eline is a woman who can take care of herself but terror pools in my gut at the thought of some-thing happening to her."

"'Eline! I'll distract him and you run.'

"'Maarten, he's a good dog. I don't think he wants to hurt me.' Tears roll down her face.

"'He's not your pet any longer. He doesn't know who you are.'

"The dog begins to viciously snap its jaw in the air at an invisible enemy. I roll my cloak around my arm like a thick bandage and creep up behind him. A stick cracks under my foot and before I can stop him the dog lunges at Eline.

"'Maarten!' she screams and dives to the left with the animal nipping at the boot of her right leg.

"My whole body lands on the dog's back with a violent crash and he falls to the ground. With my wrapped arm, I press down hard on his neck. His snout pops open in a loud whimper and he lets go of Eline. Even in his disoriented state he puts up a fight and I push harder, making sure my arms are protected from his lethal bite. One final thrust at his neck and I hear the sharp noise of bones breaking. I scramble to my feet, leaving the dog's head distorted with his neck crushed and run to Eline."

NATALIA…

"The dog comes at me. I leap away and hit the rocky ground hard. His jaw tugs at my leg. I kick and thrash at him with my other foot. It happens so fast but Maarten is on top of him and amid all the commotion I hear the dog's neck break.

"'Eline! Are you safe, my love?'

"Maarten scoops me up in his strong arms and I collapse into him. My heart is broken over the loss of a dear companion, but I'm relieved and grateful the horrible ordeal is over. 'Let me look at your leg. Did he break your skin?'

"'No. My boot saved me.'

"I turn my leg so he can see. He brushes my long dress up past my knees. At the sight of blood running down the side laces of my boot, fear crawls deep into my chest. It isn't possible. I clutch onto Maarten's chest and want him to tell me it's not really there, that my mind is playing tricks on me.

"'Maarten, I never felt him bite me. It must be from my fall.'

"'Darling, your injury may be from your fall but I won't take the chance. You know what we must do.'

"With a dread-filled nod, I acknowledge what needs to be done. I gather up my terror and hold my tears for later. If the rumors are true about what happens next, tears will be of better use to me then, than now."

MARC...

"Despair hangs around my neck like a noose. There is no time to waste. There are two deep puncture wounds on her calf above her boot. They aren't from her fall, and she and I both know it, but I don't want to scare her more than she already is. A rabid dog has bitten her. I lift her up onto the seat in the carriage and the race to save her life begins."

♨ ♨

NATALIA...

"Maarten carries me. I have my arms wrapped tight around his neck, my face nuzzled against him. His damp wool cloak smells like our barn after the rain. I hear the men shouting out their best deals in the meat market of Rue de Boucher, along with the clopping of horse and buggies through the muddy and puddle-laden dirt road. It's the noise of an ordinary day. But it's far from ordinary. Today is the day that decides whether I live or die.

"Maarten kicks open the daunting wooden doors of St. Hubert's Basilica. The rigid décor of stone and marble is as cold as the temperature inside the grand church. He places me inside one of the many deserted pews.

"'Eline, my love, wait here while I fetch *Vader* Janssens.'

"With a tender kiss he leaves. His deep voice calling for the priest echoes down the past the sanctuary into an outer area. I attend Mass here every Sunday. I come as my family did before me and as my children will continue to, a habit as common as going to the market for food.

"I lift my gaze toward the vaulted ceiling to the stained glass portrait of St. Hubert, displayed with glory above the ornate altar. He's an imposing figure and one I am proud of. Maarten's exquisite talent and hard work repaired the revered Saint's image to its original grandeur after a storm had damaged it. The glass portrays Hubert clothed in a red robe, kneeling next to a large stag. Between the deer's antler's, Jesus hangs on his cross.

"My fate lies with the beloved Bishop of Belgium, a devoted servant of a God in whom I have little, if any, faith. But St. Hubert was once like me. Would today be the day I too, have an epiphany, as Hubert had, and be given the gift of faith that, no matter how hard I search, I have yet to be blessed with?"

MARC…

"We wait in silence in a small, dully lit room. The heat from the massive fire blazing in the corner stifles the little air around us. Vader Janssen, a lanky, elderly man, dressed in the obligatory black robe, stokes the red-hot coals as sweat beads on his brow. Spread around him is various tools that, if I didn't know better, I would think his profession a blacksmith, not a humble priest. With a swipe of his arm, he wipes his moist forehead and turns to Eline. She glares with wide eyes at him and the long black poker he holds with confidence in his hand.

"Eline appears brave but I see a face laced with fear. My body is racked with terror and I pray I've made the right decision, cruel, as it may seem. I will do whatever I must to save her. She is my life.

"'Eline, my dear sister in Christ, let us pray.' Vader Janssen rests the poker inside the red glow of the coals and raises his hands in prayer. 'Today we pray to Hubert, the patron saint of hunters, hounds, and protector of rabies, for his mercy.'

"As Father continues his invocation, I reach for Eline. She huddles close to me and links her delicate hand with mine. I wish I had words to comfort her. I tell her I love her.

"'Hubert's faith was breached when he lost both his wife and son in childbirth. It wasn't until a hunting trip, that St. Peter appeared to him, warning of an impending eternity in hell, that he turned back to the Lord.' Father Janssen swings the hand censer from side to side as a thin veil of white smoke rises upward. The fragrant, spicy odor of the incense swirls around the confined space. 'St. Peter presented Hubert with a gold key and rejoiced in the knowledge that God had bestowed on him special powers against evil.'

"The priest returns the censer to its proper place and

walks toward Eline carrying a modest silver bowl of holy water. Her body stiffens and I hold her tight. He pauses in front of her, dips his thumb in the water, and makes the sign of the cross on her forehead.

"'In the name of the Father, Son, and Holy Ghost.'

"'Amen,' we say together.

"Father Janssen bows his head. 'Eline, my dear, you are in God's hands now.' He turns to me. 'Maarten, restrain her.'"

NATALIA …

"I lean back against Maarten. He wraps his strong arms around my waist trapping my own arms under his fierce grip. Like a sorcerer, a dagger magically appears from under the priest's robe and he steps closer. I dig my heels into the soft dirt floor.

"'Maarten, no, please,' I whimper, losing the last bit of courage I may have had.

"'Eline, I have you. It's the only way, my love. Trust me.'

"Without warning, the passive priest who calls himself a man of God slashes my forehead. I gasp in pain, thrashing, and kicking my legs at him to stay away. He waits for my tantrum to stop and comes at me again. His usual kind eyes harden with purpose and drive. Blood drips down past my nose and combines with the tears flowing from my eyes. Being confined, I can't wipe my face and soon the warm mixture tingles at my lips. My tongue swipes it away as a salty, coppery taste fills my mouth. I want to vomit.

"I struggle against my husband's restraints, but it's no use. I hear Father Janssen speak.

"'Angels appeared to Hubert and presented him with a stole. It's with this stole, he cured a man of rabies.'

"The old man holds a single black thread between his pointer finger and thumb. He positions the string inside the incision on my head.

"'With this simple thread from St. Hubert's holy stole and in the name of Jesus, I beseech the mercy of God to save you from the disease of rabies.'

"Maarten loosens his grip on me as the priest wraps a black bandage around my head to keep the thread in place. It must stay there for nine days. Father Janssen turns his back to me and returns to the fire. Using a poker with tongs on the end, he searches through inches of glowing ash until he finds St. Hubert's Key hidden deep in the burning coals.

"'Maarten, no more!' I plead.

"As horrible as the *cutting* was, the worst is yet to come.

"I sit on a dilapidated wooden chair, my hands

clenched on each side of the seat. It groans and creaks as I shift my body from side to side looking for a way out. The door is bolted. The keys jingle and clank on a black key ring around Father Janssen's thin waist. There is no escape.

"That's when Maarten kneels before me. At that moment, I do have an epiphany. Our love is different from others. Something old and unseen binds us together. I can't explain how or why, but of this I'm sure. He takes my hands and buries his head in my palms. I feel his warm lips on my skin, and when he gazes up at me, his eyes are swollen red, and wet, but his expression is one of pure love. He suffers with me. It's then I realize that, with him beside me, I'll get through this. Whatever God and St. Hubert's opinion of me, I'll fight with everything I have to stay here with him and my children. I cup his face with my hands, close my eyes, and nod.

"He lifts my leg onto his arm. With trembling fingers he unlaces my boot, takes it off, and removes my stocking, now stained with dried blood. Father Janssen drags over a footstool.

"'Eline, I'd rather not, but I will tie you up to keep you from lashing out,' the priest said.

"'That won't be necessary, Father. Maarten is all I need. I apologize for my earlier behavior.'

"'Very well, then, it's time.'

"Maarten rests my offending leg on the stool and

inches my dress up close to my knee. The priest turns his head. His cheeks are crimson red.

"'Father, I appreciate your chivalry, but a life or death situation has no place for modesty. Don't you agree?'

"He grunted his agreement.

"'Eline.' Maarten speaks as he sat in a chair next to me. 'I want you to look at me and nothing else. Don't take your eyes off me until it's over. Understand?'

"'Yes.'

"The poker scratches against the bottom of the hearth. When Father Janssen's tool has St. Hubert's Key firmly in the hold of its jaws, his footsteps approach. I feel the heaviness of his boney knee weighing my leg down. I clutch Maarten's chest and brace myself."

〰️ 〰️

MARC …

"I may as well be Eline's tormentor. Her agony is mine. It rips at my soul to see her in such pain, but we are fortunate to have the holy relic available to us. Victims travel from as far as Britain to receive the mark of St. Hubert's Key and be saved of rabies.

"The top of Eline's body is spiraled toward me in an awkward position, with her leg splayed out behind her.

Her wheat colored hair is tangled in the bandage around her head. A blend of blood, sweat, and dirt splatter her cheeks and chin. Her blue eyes are locked with mine and her fingers cling tightly to my shirt.

"'I grab her beautiful face with my hands and pull her near. 'Eline, don't take your eyes off me. Understand? I—'

"Father Janssen interrupts me. 'I must leave the key on while I recite *In the Name of the Father, Son and Holy Spirit, Amen.* I'll return it to the coals and place it once again on the other wound. Be strong, Eline. This is going to hurt.'

"Her skin sizzles and the sickening smell of burning flesh hits me hard. Over her head, I watch Father Janssen fan the smoke from her leg away as if he is shooing an insect aside. Eline's face distorts into a knot of pain and agony as her bottom lip quivers. Small whimpering sounds leave her mouth and tears flow freely as she weeps. 'Eline, give me your pain. Send it to me. I want to take it from you.'

"Her eyes bulge and she has my shirt taut around my neck.

"'Amen!'

"The priest's baritone voice booms. He removes the instrument of torture and Eline crumbles into me, a trembling and sobbing woman who has been through more than anyone should have to endure.

"I kiss the top of her head. Her breathing is hard and fast against me. 'Eline, my darling, we're almost there. One more. You can do it. You're strong.'

"She shakes her head frantically at me. 'No, not again.'

"Before I can console her, Father Janssen sears her leg for the second time. Eline's blood-curdling scream stays with me for me weeks."

♨ ♨

Dr. Ellis took hold of Natalia's shoulders amid her deafening shrieks. She regretted letting it go this far. She was vaguely familiar with the barbaric treatment of St. Hubert's key and shouldn't have allowed her to go through it again.

"Natalia! It's present day and you haven't been bitten. You're not in Belgium, but safe here at the vineyard with Marc and Gigi."

Natalia's stress level remained high, although her screeching subsided. She crouched over as if she were about to throw up, the teddy bear tossed on the floor, her hand clutching her calf. Dr. Ellis swore under her breath. She knew from prior experience that Marc and Natalia were not conventional patients. They relived their past lives with the same vigor and passion they experienced the first time around.

Natalia sat up, her breathing labored and sprinkled with hiccups. Her eyes were closed. "I'm sorry."

"Why would you apologize?" Relief washed over Dr. Ellis, the worst had passed and Natalia seemed to be composing herself.

She hadn't brought her back completely. Her patient was still in a semi-state of hypnosis.

She readied herself for the argument ahead. "I think you've been through enough for today."

"No, please, I—"

Dr. Ellis lifted her hand in protest. "I knew you wouldn't agree but this life is too taxing to continue. I know a little bit about St. Hubert's key and a hell of a lot about rabies. We both know how it ends. There's no need to go through the trauma again."

"You don't understand. I have to for Marc and Gigi. I'm not afraid."

"Natalia, I'm a doctor and I have to do what's best for you. I don't believe going back is in your best interest."

"I mean no disrespect, Dr. Ellis, but Marc and I promised we'd see this through to the end and that's what I'm going to do. We're friends, I trust you, and want you to take me back. I know I'll be in good hands. But, if you're not comfortable with that, I'll have Mariella find me someone who is."

"Shit," Dr. Ellis whispered.

Natalia smiled. "You've been hanging around me too me long."

"I thought you gave up cussing for Marc."

"I try. It's a hard habit to break."

Dr. Ellis relented, certain she had no chance to win in the first place. "Okay, on one condition—that you stay quasi hypnotized and rest. I'll take you deeper and we'll go back when I think you're ready."

"Agreed. Thank you."

♨ ♨

NATALIA...

"Two months pass and I remain healthy. Maarten is confident but I have my doubts. One morning I wake up to a sore throat and muscle aches. Each day it worsens but I am able to hide it from him.

"A stained glass window has broken at St. Hubert's and Maarten puts in many hours to repair it. By the end of the week, what I was afraid would happen, did."

♨ ♨

MARC...

"Two months pass and Eline shows no signs of the

horrific disease. I thank God, St. Hubert, and Vader Janssen every day for saving her.

"Our life goes on. I'm in the barn, examining the hoof of my horse that has come down with a limp. I decide there is a pebble wedged in his shoe when Alijse bursts through the door.

"'Papa! Hurry! Something's wrong with Mama. In the garden.'

"I dart past my daughter and sprint up the hill. Autumn is upon us and the day has darkened under the late-afternoon October sky. It's an ominous omen of what lies ahead.

"Eline is crumpled in a pile on the ground. Her body shudders and spasms. Vomit drips down the side of her mouth.

"'Eline.'

"I drop to my knees and slip my arms underneath her when she begins a violent attack.

"Her arms and legs thrash, battering me with unusual force.

"'Don't touch me!' she growls.

"'Eline, it's me. Maarten.'

"'Stay away from me!'

"Alijse is hysterical and steadying herself against the garden fence. 'Papa! What's wrong with her?'

"I release Eline. For a few moments, her body continues to flounder like a fish out of water, then she calms down. I take my beloved daughter, so like her mother, into my arms and hug her tight.

"'She's sick and needs our help.' I release her and give her firm instructions. 'Alijse, I need you to pull yourself together, get on your horse, and ride to Dr. Wauters. Can you do that?'

"Alijse wiped her nose on her shoulder and inhaled deeply. 'Yes, I'll do anything to help Mama.'

"'I know, sweetheart. Now, go, hurry!'

"As she stumbles off to the barn, still sniffling, I let my mind wander. It can't be. Eline's been healthy. Her wound healed, leaving only a minimal scar. I fight a silent battle until I convince myself it's something else, something that would pass."

NATALIA...

"My brain is garbled and confused. I can't keep a straight thought. I'm agitated and restless. I know I love, him...Maa...Maarten, but the thought of him touching me is horrifying. A girl is crying. Alijse, I think, is her name. While I want to comfort her, she irritates me and I want her to stop the incessant whining. Pain stabs at my stomach and my legs twist with sporadic tremors. I don't know what's wrong with me or why my mind is muddled, but I would give anything to crawl out of my skin and die."

☙☙

MARC…

"I plead with Dr. Wauters for answers. 'Why has God turned his back on Eline?'

"He is a man of large stature, middle-aged with spectacles and a kind personality. He and I talk outside of our bedroom. The door is cracked open and I pace back and forth so I can see her. She is calmer but delirious, rambling on about things I don't recognize.

"'Maarten, listen to me. God has turned his back on no one. This isn't God's fault or his place to cure it. It's a human affliction as old as the ancient Greeks and therefore, we need to find a way to treat it.'

"'We arrived at St. Hubert's within an hour of the bite. I don't understand. I've heard about all the miracles performed on behalf of St. Hubert's key. I've failed her.'

"'Horseshit, Maarten. You're a good man and Eline is a wonderful woman. I've been called to care for their so-called miracles. I haven't documented one true case of a cure from the branding. It's nothing more than a dangerous, archaic, religious superstition. People won't allow science to help them as long as the church tells them their ways work better. It does nothing but give them false hope.'

"'Are you not a man of God, Dr. Wauters?'"

"'Yes, of course, but I'm also a man of science. I believe they both have important roles in our lives.'

"I sit in Eline's favorite chair and hold my head. 'Is she going to die?'

"Dr. Wauters lays a gentle hand on my shoulder, 'I'm sorry.'

"'How long do I have with her?'

"'When did her symptoms begin?'

"'Today.'

"'No, she's been sick all week. She didn't want to worry Papa.' Alijse's soft voice comes from across the room.

"'Alijse, sweetheart, this is adult business and not for young ears.'

"'No, Papa, I'm fifteen and she's my mother. I have a right to know. I want to know.' She remains defiant with her arms crossed over her chest.

"'I am your father and I am asking you to leave. I will tell you what you need to know.' Alijse doesn't move. 'Now!'

"I hate to take a harsh tone with her but I do what I must. She stomps out of the room.

"My world is spinning out of control. I don't know what to do. I need Eline. What will I do without her? In desperation, I reach for a bottle of gin, pour two glasses, and hand one to Dr. Wauters. I gulp mine while the good doctor sips his and tells me of the vile death by rabies.

"'I'm sorry, Maarten, this will be hard to hear but it's best that you know what to expect. Besides the hallucinations, delirium, and violent outbursts, there are two things I must warn you of. First is Hydrophobia, the fear of water, which is common in most patients. Just the sight of it can cause panic.

"Pray God takes her quick or she may well die of thirst.'

"He finished what remained of his gin and continued. 'Two, in what I believe is the cruelest aspect, is that all of that may subside and Eline will have a time of clarity. It's during this period when she'll understand what is happening to her. It's tragic but don't be fooled into thinking she's cured and has come back to you. She hasn't.'

"'You're a merciless son of a bitch, aren't you?'

"'I've been called worse. I'm a realist and believe you'll be better off knowing what's to come.'

"He pulled on his cloak, sat his hat on top of his head, and walked to the door.

"'Send for me if you need anything at all. I'll come as soon as I can.'"

♨ ♨

MARC…

"Days go by and exhaustion settles deep in my bones. Eline suffers from insomnia amid her incoherent rants and neither of us sleep. I refuse to leave her side. There is a knock on the door. It's Alijse with food and drink.

"'Good morning, Mama, how are you today?'

"'Alijse, it's not wise for you to come in.'

"I don't want Eline to scare her. Her mother's once beautiful hair is dry as straw, dirty, and matted. She stares blankly at the wall, muttering. She has no control of her bladder and smells of piss, although she no longer drinks or eats.

"I try to wash her, but like Dr. Wauters predicted, the sight of water in the basin sends her into a violent assault. Her face is thin and shallow, and her lips are cracked and brittle as her hair.

"'Papa, stop treating me as a child. I want to see her.' Alijse walks in and stops mid-step.

She goes still as a statue at the sight of her mother. Her eyes fill with tears but she sits on the edge of the bed.

Eline looks into the distance and mumbles, 'The stones are lining up. The stones are lining up.'

"'Alijse, are you all right?' She nods. 'Stay with her while I get a clean blanket.'

"I am only gone a moment but when I get back, it's too late.

'Alijse, no!'

"Alijse holds a cup of water to Eline's parched mouth. Her whole body rebels in fear as she jerks and convulses. She doesn't take a sip but she gags and retches.

"'Mama, you must drink.'

"In a fierce outburst, Eline smacks the cup away and pushes Alijse onto the floor. 'Leave me alone!'

"I rush to Alijse's side and help her to her feet. 'Sweetheart, she doesn't know what she's doing.'

"Before Alijse can answer, Eline begins to screech like a wounded animal. 'Help me. Get them off me. They're crawling and biting.'

"She digs at her arms, neck, and face like a woman possessed. 'Spiders, everywhere, don't you see them? Help me!'

Her scratches break her skin and blood trickles down to the top of her white nightdress.

"'Alijse, leave. You don't need to see this.'

"'I love her, too. We must stop her from hurting herself. You can't do it alone.'

"'I know. I'm so sorry. Get a sheet and rip it into strips. I'll hold her down and you tie her wrists to the bed tight as you can. I can tighten them afterward.'

"With clenched fists, Eline beats at me. Thank God,

I prevent her from striking our daughter. The horrifying ordeal of restraining Eline is soon over. Alijse and I huddle in the corner of the room, sharing a desperate embrace. In the background, Eline's cries of agony drown out our own sobs of grief."

♨ ♨

NATALIA…

"My arms are spread open and my shoulders are on fire. I try to sit up but something tugs on my wrists. They are sore, chapped. Faint memories invade my mind. Chaos, crying, and violence.

"The room is dark except for the pale glow of Maarten's lantern lit on the nightstand. I see the shadowed contour of his profile. His shoulders are hunched over and his head rests on his arms on the table.

"'Maarten.' My throat burns with thirst as I speak. 'Maarten, may I have some water, please?'

"'Eline? Eline, is it really you?' He hurries to the bed and raises a glass to my lips. 'Of course, my love.'

"'I'm parched but I can't…swallow.'

"'Of course, my love.'"

He removes a handkerchief from his pocket, hurries to the water basin, and submerges it. He sits on the bed next to me and holds the dripping cloth to my lips. I open my mouth and he moves it inside onto my tongue. The cool liquid is like an oasis to my desert mouth. Maarten, always so gentle and loving. I will miss him with my whole heart.

"'Thank you.' The dim light reveals a bruise on his cheek. 'What happened to your face?'

"'Nothing. It's not important. I'm so glad to see you.'

"'Did I do that to you?' He doesn't answer. 'Did I hurt Alijse?' Alarm shakes me at the fear I've harmed my baby.

"'No, you would never hurt her.'

"'I hate what I've become.'

"'It's not your fault. I'll love you no matter what. Let me untie you.'

"'I wouldn't.'

"His face twisted in anguish. 'Eline, I've missed you.' His warm body curls up next to mine. I want nothing more than to wrap my arms around him and never let him go. But that is impossible. I am grateful to have him near, to feel him, smell him, and take one last memory of him with me. 'Eline, I need you. You said we'd be together forever.'

"'Maarten, I'll love you forever and you will be in my heart even when we are separated.'

"'Don't leave me.'

"'Maarten, please, listen. I need you to end this for

me. I don't want to go back to that horrible place in my mind. I can't, please don't make me.'

"I have no right to ask such a thing of him, but I could endure no more.

"'Eline, I…I can't. Don't speak of such things.'

"'Maarten, if you love me, let me go. We're both suffering and there's no need.'

"He continued his refusal but his words slurred as the blackness overtook my thoughts. 'Maa…Maarten …love.'

"There's an unbearable ringing in my ears and Maarten is fading. I try to hold on to him. I don't want to lose him, but it's stronger than I am."

〰 〰

MARC…

"'Eline, come back!'

"It's no use. She's gone. The barren look on her face has returned. She fights against her bindings and her mouth salivates.

"She's screaming, 'Stop the God damn church bells. I can't stand the noise. The ringing. Make it go away.'

"I stand there, the most helpless man in the world, as my love slams her head against the headboard over and over.

"Harder and harder she rams it but gets no relief from the demons haunting her.

"The pillow is clenched in my fingers. 'Eline, stop, my love, please.' She continues to yell and smash her head. I don't know what do, how to help her. Her hair is a bloody, matted mess. 'Eline, stop it, Eline!' She lets out one last muffled cry through the pillow smothering her face. "Eline, please.' Her body struggles beneath me. I push harder as snot and tears drip on my hands. 'Stop, Eline.'

"And she does."

♨ ♨

NATALIA...

"I'm at peace."

♨ ♨

MARC...

"She's still with death. She has no heartbeat, no breath, no life inside her. I untie her and lay with her in the bed we shared for so many years. 'Eline, what am I to do now? You promised me forever.'

"Time goes by.

"The warmth of Eline's body is gone. Her stiff hand lays in mine, but I don't move.

"'Papa!' Alijse has her hand over her mouth. 'Mama?'

"'I'm sorry, darling.'

"I'm drowning in an ocean of guilt at what I've done to both my wife and daughter. Alijse must never find out.

"'I didn't say goodbye.'

"I fumble for words. 'She wouldn't have wanted you to see her at the end. She loved you very much. Come lay with us.'

"Alijse crawls in next to her mother, nestles her head in her chest, and weeps like a baby. My soul is numb and empty. I don't know what to say next. So I speak the truth. 'Alijse, I'm scared.'

"'Don't worry, Papa, I'll take care of you.'

♨ ♨

"It's the dead of winter. I've been alone four months. I stumble to the front of our home and look in the window. Alijse sits at the table with a plate of food in front of her. There is another plate across from her. For me.

"I reek of sex and cheap perfume. I'm drunk and have betrayed Eline and our love.

"I refuse to have Alijse see me like this. She'll hate me. I hate myself.

"Ashamed, I continue back down the dark path to town."

♨ ♨

"I pause in front of Alijse's door. She still cries for Eline, two years after I took her mother away from her. The distance between us is as long as the River Zenne. I can't look at her.

"She has grown into a beautiful, young woman, head strong, vibrant, and full of life—a living image of Eline. She is seventeen now, time for a husband.

"'Papa, you wanted to see me?'

"I pour myself a drink from a bottle of gin, my constant companion of late. 'Yes. I want to talk to you.'

"'I have something to say to you as well. Sander Lefabvre has asked me to marry him and I'm happy to do so.'

"I spit out my drink and slam the glass on the table. 'The butcher's son? I forbid it. I've already betrothed you to Jasper Pieters. The dowry has been paid. The date has been set.'

"'I refuse. I love Sander and he loves me. The way you and mama loved each other. She always told me how great your love was and hoped I'd find the same some day. I have.'

"'Ha! Your mother lied. To marry for love is a foolish fairy tale. It will do nothing but leave you broken. You will marry Jasper and he will provide your every need and then you will be happy. I'm your father. I know what's best for you.'

"She leans in close to me. Her hands are firm on the table and her expression brims with anger. 'How do know you what's best for me when you don't even know me? You go from work, to brothel, then home to your bottle. I understand there's a whore you fancy in particular because she looks like Mama. But any whore will do, won't she?'

"I don't realize what I have done until I feel the sting on my palm and the red welt rises on her cheek. She doesn't flinch. 'How dare you speak to me with such disrespect? You will do as I say and marry Jasper.'

"'No, Papa, I'll do as I please.'

"'Get out!'

"The next day Alijse is gone. She scribbles a brief note saying her life is with Sander now. I should go after her. Try to make things right. But I don't. I'm gutless. It's easier to grab my bottle and bury myself in Britta's delightful bosom. Britta allows me the opportunity, if only in my intoxicated imagination, to once again be with Eline."

♨ ♨

"My fever burns high. My chest is heavy with consumption. Father Janssen passed years ago. Father Hermans visits me.

"'Maarten, under the circumstances, I took it upon myself to send word to your daughter about your condition. She's here with me today. You have two grandchildren, a boy and a girl.'

"I feel nothing at Father Hermans words. My heart has turned as cold as the headstone that will soon mark my grave. Amid a coughing fit I say, 'Send her away. She's as dead to me as Eline.'

"Soon after, death takes me and I never see Alijse again."

Chapter 7

We are one, after all, you and I, together we suffer, together exist and forever will recreate each other.
~Pierre Teilhard de Chardin,
French Philosopher 1881-1955

Marc drew the drapes closed and sprawled out diagonally across the king-size bed. On his back, he stared into the darkness as the door creaked open. A triangle of light formed on the ceiling and Natalia's oblong silhouette moved toward him.

She slid next to him and rested her hand on his stomach. "Hey baby, are you all right?"

"I don't know."

What he did know was he needed her, full of life,

next to him. As he came out of his regression, Dr. Collier saw how shaken he was and promised him everyone he loved was here with him.

The logical part of him knew that but this past life hit him harder than any other ever had. The small illogical part of him needed reassurance.

He rolled over and buried his head on the right side of her chest, savoring each rise and fall of her breath. She smelled of yeast, fermenting wine, and Gigi's shampoo. It was pure Natalia, alive and filled with the everyday aroma of their life together.

As she wrapped her arms around him, the dread and regrets haunting him diminished.

"There is no need to torture yourself like this." Natalia pulled him closer. There were love and comfort in her words, but it did nothing to change his grim mood. "Gigi loves you."

"I can't believe I turned my back on her like that. What kind of person am I? She'll never forgive me."

"She's forgiven both of us," Natalia stroked his hair. "That's why she fought so hard for us to be together to be a family again. She's telling us we need to forgive ourselves."

"I couldn't even look at her." Marc twisted out of her arms, sat up, and rubbed his tired eyes. "She reminded me so much of you. She looked like you, talked like you, and lived with your passion. It was too much."

"I know. Mariella let me hear your recording."

Marc dropped his hands to his side. "You!"

With Natalia safe and well, a darker emotion crept through him.

"Me?" Natalia reached out for him but he jerked away from her.

"Do you know how hard it is to hear your own child cry for her mother, knowing you're the one who took her away in the first place?" He flung his legs over the side of the bed and sat on the edge with his stiff back to her. "Don't ever ask me to do something like that again. It almost killed me. I wasn't the same after that."

The bedsprings bounced as she crawled over to him. She squeezed the top of his arms and kissed the back of his head.

"You did what I asked. You set me free and gave me peace. It was a courageous thing to do and you did it because you loved me." Her voice cracked. "I would have died a long, drawn out and painful death. You saved me and I love you for it."

"She never got to say good-bye," Marc snapped and started to get up.

"I'm sorry." Natalia gently pulled him back on the bed and massaged his neck and shoulders. "I didn't want her to see me like that, did you? I wasn't her mother any more. I was a screaming, raving lunatic."

"You don't understand the consequences!" He broke

free, stood up, and faced her. "Your selfishness and need to always have what you want left behind two devastated people who were lost. Instead of helping each other, we hurt each other."

Natalia's posture straightened and her face lost any trace of empathy.

He expected her reaction. One of the many layers of her strong will was defiance.

She would defend her actions to the end, under any circumstance, if she believed them to be right.

"I'm sorry you feel that way," she said. "I may as well tell you now that I've had a living will for a long time and was going to ask you to replace Robbie's signature. I refuse to be hooked up to a machine that feeds me and pees for me. I want quality of life not quantity." She hopped off the bed and stood rigid in front of him. "If you have a problem with that and won't sign, I'll keep my brother on."

"See, this is what I mean. I'm having a hard time and, instead of helping me everything gets turned back to you." He pushed his finger into her chest. "Doesn't it?"

Natalia swiped his hand down. "You were an adult with a child and responsibilities. I can't help that you made bad choices after I was gone."

Marc inched closer and his body loomed over hers. "Do you know what life lesson you need to learn? That everything isn't about you."

"That may be, but this regression was your idea. Next time pick your door more carefully."

He stomped to their bedroom door and flung it open. "I'm sure about this door."

He stepped into the hallway. When Natalia started to follow, he firmly shut the door, creating a barrier between them.

As he moved down the hall, it amazed him how close they were last night and how far apart they were now.

♨ ♨

It was six-thirty and Marc had spent the last hour upstairs with Gigi. Natalia was setting the table when he appeared with their little girl in his arms. Natalia opened the oven and checked on the garlic bread and chicken Parmesan. "I'm heating up dinner."

"We're going out for a while."

"Okay. I can save this for tomorrow." She reached in and pulled out the hot food. "Let me get my sweater. Gigi can't be gone that long. She'll need to nurse."

"No. I'll grab one of the bottles of your milk from the refrigerator." He shot her a patronizing glance. "Believe it or not, we'll both survive without you."

Her temper in full throttle mode, Natalia banged the casserole dish on the stove. She swallowed a mouthful of obscenities and calmly replied, "Fine. You're hands are full. Let me get the door for you."

Natalia ate her dinner with a heaping of self-pity and a side dish of wounded ego. Marc left without kissing her good-bye. He'd never done that before. The last time they were regressed, it brought them together. This time it was ripping them apart. She vowed to never revisit a past life again.

As she cleaned up, her breasts filled with a familiar heaviness. It was eight o'clock, time to nurse Gigi. She'd have to use that vile machine, the breast pump. After Natalia accomplished the awkward task, she fell onto the couch with a blanket and remote in hand. Blaring from the TV was a reality show about divorce court. Too tired to turn the channel, she let it play.

It was the most ridiculous thing she'd ever seen. She knew a real court and judge would never allow the silly antics to go on.

It was for pure entertainment and shock value. With the long, emotional day taking its toll, she lost interest, closed her eyes, and drifted asleep...

♨ ♨

Natalia and Marc were moving fast. He held her hand, not with affection, only to drag her along behind him. A dim glow illuminated their path. They floated through a misty fog, but unlike fog they could see what was ahead of them. She had no idea where they were or where they were going. Marc hadn't spoken to her since he told her she was coming with him.

They came upon two intimidating wooden doors framed within a large fieldstone arch. Hung up high, a rusty doorknocker, molded into a tortured soul's face, stared down at them.

Even at six-feet, Marc had trouble reaching the round piece. With the tips of his fingers, he lifted it and let it drop against the metal nailed to the door. It clanked once with a thunderous boom.

The door scraped across the floor with a horrible grating noise as a woman dragged it open.

Natalia got the sense she was an ancient being, but her face was ageless. Her long, flowing hair was the colors of the rainbow.

Her oval eyes were the color of black opals and her height was substantial. She towered over Marc and, unlike him, would have no trouble using the doorknocker. Instead of being afraid, Natalia was mesmerized.

"Do you have an appointment?" The pitch of her voice was annoyingly high.

Marc nodded. "Yes." The woman placed her hand on his chest and peered deep into his eyes. "Hey! What are you doing?"

"Relax. Your eyes are the windows to your soul.

This is how I can identify you." She released him and an empty clipboard materialized in her hands. "This time you are called Marcos Tremonti, correct?"

"Yes."

"A clipboard?" Natalia asked.

The woman ignored her and began to shuffle through papers that were not there a second ago.

Next, the woman turned to Natalia and bore black eyes deep into hers. "Natalia Santagario?"

"Yes."

The woman continued to look at her papers and directed the conversation to Marc. "It says here you are Twin Flames."

"Yes," he said.

"Well—" She threw her arms up into the air and the clipboard disappeared in a puff of smoke. "—this complicates things. Are you *sure* you want to do this? I can count on one hand how many Twin Flames have done this since the beginning of time. It is highly unusual."

"Natalia is highly unusual." Marc took a small step closer to the woman. "Please," he begged, "I need to do this."

She waved a long, bony finger at him. "Once it's done, there is no going back."

"I understand."

"As you wish."

The woman spun around in an eruption of color that

reminded Natalia of the spin art machine at a carnival. The next thing she knew they were whisked inside her multi-hued whirlwind and dropped down in a small, sparsely furnished room. There was a beautifully crafted mahogany desk on a platform.

On each side of the desk were two, small lit candelabrums. A long flame ran down from both candlesticks and burned across the top of the desk.

In the middle, the fire spiraled upward together to form one larger blaze.

"Marc, please tell me what's going on."

"Shh," he said without looking at her.

"Don't shush me. I have a right to know—"

There was a loud snap and a bright flash of light. A man dressed in a white robe approached them. The complete opposite of the woman at the door, his stature was small and his spiked hair was a single vibrant red.

"I'm Ophiuchus," he said but offered no hand of welcome. "This is my dear assistant, Cassiopeia." He shot the multi-colored-haired woman a tender glance. "Please have a seat."

He pointed to two stiff and uncomfortable looking chairs.

Natalia and Marc sat as Ophiuchus made his way behind his desk.

"Welcome to Soul Severance and Separation Services. I say welcome with a heavy heart because I am always saddened when one soul wants to sever itself from another.

"But I also understand eternity is a long time and sometimes these things just don't work out. It becomes impossible to learn your life lessons with each incarnation if you're being dragged down by a soul mate who you can no longer get along with."

He moved his chair back, smoothed out the back of his robe and sat down. "However, I'm especially dismayed today because of your status. Twin Flame soul mates usually pass the test of time, but alas, every once in awhile, these too fall apart."

Natalia bolted up from her chair. "Excuse me. I don't know what you're talking about. I don't want to sever my soul from Marc's. This is a huge mistake."

Ophiuchus folded his hands in front of him. "Maybe you don't, my dear, but Marcos does. Do you always believe everything is about you?"

"Yes, sir, she does," Marc answered before she could speak for herself.

"I do not!" Natalia twisted her whole body to face Marc. "What's going on?"

"I'm sorry, but it's time," he said. "You're too difficult and I'm exhausted. I don't think I can go another round with you."

Natalia lowered herself back into her chair as Marc's words erupted throughout her entire being, leaving her mind reeling. She snapped to attention as Ophiuchus forcefully clapped his hands together twice.

Four young men clad in tunics struggled to carry out the largest book Natalia had ever seen.

The book was antediluvian, its gold binding barely holding together.

With a grunt, they lifted it over their heads and plopped it on Ophiuchus' desk. A plume of dust flared into the man's face, causing him to cough.

He cleared the air with a wave of his hand and opened it with ease.

"A giant book? You've got to be kidding." The absurdity of the situation made her giggle. "Is that the permanent record of our lives? It is the twenty first century you know, how about you computerize?"

Ophiuchus opened a small case and took out a pair of glasses. He rubbed them clean on his robe and slipped them on. "Marcos, is she always like this?"

"Yes, sir. I'm afraid so."

"No, I'm not! I just don't understand what's going on." Natalia raised her voice.

Ignoring her outburst, Ophiuchus carefully turned one yellowed page after another. When he found what he was looking for, he moved his pointer finger down the page and stopped.

"Oh yes, here we are. Natalia Santagario. My, my, my, you have quite a list here. Among other things, it says you are uncompromisingly strong-willed, have a dreadful temper, and an even fouler mouth. It mentions general immaturity and says that you say and do what you want, whenever you want."

His eyes looked away from the page and to Natalia. "How do you plead?"

"Not true," Natalia stammered. "Well…maybe…sometimes, but not all the time."

"Here's an interesting tidbit." He pushed his glasses farther up on his nose. "Adulterer."

"What?" Natalia crossed her arms as guilt nagged her over the one night she and Marc spent together before he was divorced. It was always with her. It never left. "That's not fair. It's on his list too, you know!"

"I'm afraid this isn't about Marcos's list, but yours." He slammed the book shut.

"You just said everything *wasn't* about me. Make up your damn mind."

"You'd try the patience of a saint, wouldn't you, Ms. Santagario? Let's move on," Ophiuchus said.

"No, we're not moving on." Natalia jumped up from her seat again and paced in front of Ophiuchus' desk. "Who the hell's in charge here? That's who I want to see. Who or what decided we were going to be Twin Flames to begin with? Who connected our souls? I think they have some responsibility here."

"That's not possible." Ophiuchus shook his head.

"That's not the way our Soular System works. No one sees Soular Plexus. He's far too busy."

"Solar System? *He*? So, men run the universe as well, huh? Great! Isn't the Solar Plexus a bunch of nerves that run to your abdomen?" Natalia laughed. "Okay, Marc, let's go. This is either a bad joke or a very bad dream. I know we had a fight today but we'll figure it out as soon as I wake up."

"Cassiopeia!" the robed man called out and she obediently glided in front of Natalia blocking her way. "Not that I have to explain anything to you, but I'm speaking of *Soul*ar Plexus. Plexus is from the Latin word meaning *braid*. Latin was our language, but we let you humans borrow it and you took a particular liking to it. Soular Plexus connects the souls by standing in the middle and braiding the two souls and himself together. He then rises out from between them leaving them entwined. That's his job, this is mine."

"Busy, my ass," Natalia mumbled. "He should be here."

"Sit down." Cassiopeia ordered and Natalia involuntarily fell back into her seat.

"Enough!" Ophiuchus slammed his fists hard down on the desk. He stood and walked over to Marc. "You poor lad, how have you been able to put up with this for so long?"

"I drink a lot," Marc admitted.

"Well, I can certainly understand that. The good news is there are many other soul mates to choose from."

Ophiuchus snapped his fingers. Like the opening of a Broadway show, a spotlight shone down on a glistening stage revealing a chorus line of women, each one more beautiful and sexier than the next, all scantily dressed, their voluptuous bodies on display.

The corner of Marc's mouth curled into a lustful grin as he ogled the women parading their goods in front of him while a symphony of sultry music played in the background.

Natalia tried to get up from her chair but couldn't move. Cassiopeia wasn't touching her, yet somehow restrained her.

"Ophiuchus," Cassiopeia said, "don't forget the birthmark."

"Oh, yes, thank you, my dear." The man stood directly behind Marc and rested his open palms on Marc's left shoulder. "This is going to be uncomfortable. Actually, it's going to hurt like hell but if you want to be severed, the birthmark has to go. I must remove it from your soul as well as your physical body. I can only do it with your permission."

"Please, Marc, don't do it," Natalia pleaded.

Marc nodded his head in the affirmative to the man.

"Very well then. Ladies."

At Ophiuchus' direction, two women floated to

Marc, each taking a turn to wrap their arms around his neck, presenting him with a close-up view of their well-endowed cleavage, then sat on either side of him.

They each grabbed one of Marc's hands and held them tight.

"I'm sorry, son. Brace yourself."

Marc's head dropped and his jaw clenched as he grimaced with pain. He squeezed the women's hands until his knuckles turned white. They took the strength of his grip without flinching.

Natalia fought against her invisible bindings, rocking back and forth in the chair.

"Stop it! You're hurting him," she screamed. "Marc! I'll do whatever you want. Please, don't hurt him anymore!"

Ophiuchus removed his hands and Marc collapsed into the women's welcoming arms.

"Is it gone?" Natalia whispered.

"Yes, I'm afraid it's gone forever," Ophiuchus said.

"Let me see."

"There is no need. I can assure you it's gone."

"I said let me see," Natalia demanded. "Don't fuck with me right now. I have nothing to lose."

Ophiuchus relented with a nod of his head and the two women pulled Marc's shirt over his head. Natalia tried to grab a sip of breath, but couldn't.

It was gone. There was no birthmark or tattoo, just

his clear, beautiful olive skin. No pox marks, no red wine stain, no snakebites. What had brought them together was no more. *They* were no more.

It would be easy to break down, but she refused to give Marc the satisfaction. If this is what he wanted, so be it. She'd fall apart later, by herself.

"There is one more thing," Ophiuchus said with a solemn bow of his head. "Marcos, come with me." Marc rose to his feet and the two women escorted him to the desk with the spiral flame. "In order to completely sever a Twin Flame soul mate, the flame that was lit at your creation must be extinguished. Marcos, it has to be you."

Natalia had never felt so helpless.

A piece of her died every second Marc came closer to his goal of ripping his soul from hers.

As hard as she tried, she couldn't stop the tears from streaming down her cheeks.

Her body trembled and she screamed, "*No!*" as Marc leaned over and blew out the flame.

CHAPTER 8

Are you strong enough to be my man?
~ *Sheryl Crow lyrics*

Natalia awoke with a gasp, curled in the fetal position with her fists clenched. Fear fluttered in her stomach. She was in a cold sweat. Her tears caused her hair to stick to her face like glue.

She whipped the blanket off and went into the kitchen. Gigi's diaper bag sat on the counter and her empty bottle lay in the sink. It was ten o'clock.

Damn him!

She opened the top left cabinet, reached for the bottle of Maker's Mark, and poured a shot.

Nine months of pregnancy and six weeks of recovery had passed since she last felt the tingling sensation of the Kentucky whiskey on her tongue.

Natalia licked her lips and took a sip, letting it swish around in her mouth before she swallowed. Its smooth, oak taste warmed her soul. She poured another shot and downed it in one gulp.

An irritating voice in her head cautioned her to take a minute to calm down and get her thoughts together before she went upstairs. But that wasn't how she was wired. With one rude, telepathic, *Shut the fuck up*, the voice went silent and she was climbing the stairs two at a time.

Natalia flew into their bedroom to find Marc and Gigi sound asleep on the bed. She removed a plush cushion from the chair in the corner and tossed it on the floor. Careful not to wake Gigi, she lifted her off the bed and placed her on the cushion.

With a tender kiss she said, "I'm sorry sweetie, but Daddy and I have a few things to talk about."

She crawled on the bed and rattled him with a solid shove. "Marc, wake up!"

He twitched, moaned a refusal, and rolled over toward the edge.

Natalia gave him one final shake, harder than she intended, and he tumbled off the side, landing with a thump.

He sat up in a slow, sleepy daze.

"Nat, what the hell?" His head angled to the top of the bed. "Where's Gigi?"

Natalia lay on her belly and peered over the edge of the bed at him. "She's asleep over there. Take off your shirt."

"What? No. If you think getting thrown out of bed turns me on, you're wrong."

"Don't be such a sore ass. It was an accident." She offered him her hand and helped him up. "Now take off your shirt."

Face to face with Marc, her red puffy eyes gave her away. "Nat, have you been crying?"

"I want to see your birthmark."

If Marc were still hers, he couldn't deny her, no matter how upset he was. His birthmark was their bond, their strength *and* their weakness.

"You don't fight fair," he muttered under his breath and yanked the shirt over his head.

He held his ground, not turning his back to her, instead making her walk behind him.

The moment Natalia saw it, she whimpered in relief. All the marks were there as well as the beautiful Twin Flame tattoo that surrounded it.

With a shaky finger she touched it. Unable to control herself, she began to sob.

Marc spun around to face her, his expression and his body relaxed and mellow.

"Hey, Gigi and I had a long talk this evening. Well, I did most of the talking, but I told her how sorry I was and that things will be different this time."

He took a step closer. "She thought maybe I owed you an apology. So I'm, um, sorry, you know, about this afternoon."

He rocked back and forth with his hands in his sweat pockets. "I shouldn't have been so hard on you. It all hit me so fast and I didn't handle it well. It wasn't right to take something out on you that happened a long time ago."

He reached down and grabbed her hands. "You don't cry often. That wasn't my intention."

"I know." Natalia grabbed a tissue from the box on the nightstand and wiped her eyes. "We've been out of sync lately, don't you think?"

"I thought we were in perfect sync last night." He gave her a playful wink. "Nat, we have a new baby and life we're adjusting to. Things are bound to be upside down for a while."

"Do I make life difficult for you?"

"Come on, let's sit down." He plopped down on the bed and she followed. "Life is hard on its own. You make it a bit more…ah…interesting. But on the upside, it's never boring. I'll give you that."

"You left without kissing me goodbye tonight. You've never done that before."

"You didn't kiss my birthmark a few minutes ago. You've never done that before."

Her body sagged in a dismal realization. Her eyes filled up again.

"Maybe we are at the end of our time together."

"Why would you say something like that? Baby, what's wrong?" He slipped his arms around her waist and drew her close.

She eased into his chest, the touch of his warm, bare skin soothing.

"I've never seen you like this," he said. "I really am sorry about before. You believe me, don't you?"

"Yes, of course. I had a terrible dream."

She pulled away and told him how he wanted to send their souls to Splitsville. He listened attentively, although on occasion, he looked both amused and incredulous.

"Then—" She jumped to her feet and stood with her hands on her hips. "—you blew out the candle." She snapped her fingers. "Just like that. You didn't look at me, or say you were sorry or anything. Poof. It was out and we were over."

"Wow. That sounds like a nightmare, except for one part." He flashed her a mischievous grin. "Could we recap about the hot women I could choose from?"

She pushed him onto his back on the bed. "I'm not in the mood for your stupid-ass jokes, right now."

"It was a bad dream," he said as he sat up. "I know for sure there's no such thing as a Soul Severance Tribunal or whatever you called it."

"What makes you so sure?"

"Because if there was I would have done it at least six lives ago."

"I'm glad you think you're funny." She spun on her heels and marched to the door while he laughed at his own joke. "I thought we could have a serious conversation."

"Okay, okay, wait." He ran after her. "I swear no more teasing." This time when he wrapped his arms around her, he held her tight against him and didn't let her go, even though she fought to get free. "Why are you letting this dream bother you so much?"

She continued to squirm in his arms. "He said I was too strong willed."

"Nat, stop it. You are, but I wouldn't have it any other way. I've been handling your personality for quite some time. I consider myself an expert. I can take anything you throw at me. I might get pissed, but I can take it."

She gave up the fight to break away. "I thought when you found your soul mate you were perfect for each other. That life would be wonderful and easy and we'd always see eye to eye on everything."

"Baby, listen to me." He ran his thumb over her lips.

"We are perfect for each other, but that doesn't mean we're perfect. We're still human beings with feelings and emotions. We get angry, hurt, happy, and sad, but most important, we screw up." He kissed the top of her head. "I don't know how we'll end. Maybe we'll cease to exist at some point. But I do know when the time comes, we'll end like we started so long ago, together."

Damn it, she hated the rare occasion when she couldn't control the water works. "Promise?"

"I promise." His mouth fell hard on hers with a sweet urgency as his tongue danced around her mouth, tasting her, wanting her, and leaving her burning with desire. "Been in the whiskey, huh? After the day we had, I could have used a shot too, you know."

This time she gave him a small smile. "Sorry."

"I need you, Nat, I'm a mess without you. Didn't this past life prove that?"

Natalia pivoted him around so he faced the wall. She ran the palms of her hands up his strong back. On her toes, she kissed his birthmark. "I need you, too. Together, forever," she said as if sealing a sacred pact.

He reached behind and slid her arms around his waist. "Yes, baby, together, forever."

Gigi snuggled close between her sleeping parents,

bound together in this life by their love for each other. The inevitable was upon her. Soon she would begin to forget. The memories would seem far away at first, then become dimmer as she relearned the ways of life—then one day they'd be gone. She'd start over with a clean slate, the way it was meant to be.

Gigi had had one more thing to take care of before she returned, but time had run out.

Now it would fall on Marc and Natalia. Their love would be tested once again in what might be their hardest challenge yet.

THE END

BLURB

She'd never met him before...or had she?

The last thing forty-year-old Natalia Santagario expected was to be sitting on a Manhattan barstool, ogling a man she's never met, but swears she knows.

He didn't know her at all...or did he?

The mysterious dark-haired woman at the end of the bar stops twenty-eight-year old Marc Tremonti in his tracks. His head says she's a stranger, but his heart tells him otherwise.

Together they embark on an adventure that will change their lives forever.

Marc's aunt Mariella, an expert in reincarnation, persuades them to relive their past to explain their enigmatic attraction. As they open the doors to their past lives, they discover they have been lovers for hundreds of lives, are connected by an ancient bond, and are considered Twin Flame soul mates.

But their reunion in this life is complicated by an almost ex-wife, a temporary bout of amnesia, and a mischievous and meddling ghost with its own agenda.

Will their strong connection find a way to bring them together? Or is this the lifetime where they must go their separate ways?

EXCERPT

Marc didn't remember a thing after the accident...not even her.

Natalia made it from her hospital room to Marc's without the nurses noticing. She tiptoed over to his bed and softly said,

"Hello." If he *was* asleep, it shouldn't wake him.

He rolled over—and stared at her. It felt as if a tsunami had crashed over her. Her legs shook so bad, she didn't think they would hold her up. Stumbling backward, she leaned against the wall so she wouldn't fall down.

"Are you okay?" he asked. "Do you want me to call the nurse?"

"No," she squeaked out. "I'm sorry. I should go."

"No. Wait, please come here."

She couldn't put one foot in front of the other, so she just stood there.

"You took the trouble to come to my room, why won't you come in? Who are you?"

"My name is Natalia."

He continued to stare. "You know, out of all the people who've come in here, you're the only one who seems familiar to me. Do I know you?"

"We were in the cab together when it had the accident."

"Oh. I'm sorry. Are you okay?"

She tried to pull herself together. The last thing she wanted was for him to see her like this. "I think I'm a little better than you."

"So, you know me. How about my wife?"

"I know your Aunt Mariella. I've never met you

wife." She wasn't up to spending any more time with him and wanted to leave before she burst into tears. "Well, good night. I just wanted to see how you were."

"Will you come back and visit me again? I would like you to tell me how we know each other."

"I don't know. I'll try." She wasn't even out the door before the tears ran down her cheeks. The real sobbing didn't start until she was in back in her bed, alone in the dark.

About the Author

Debbie Christiana loves to read and write about mysteries, unusual love stories, and things that go bump in the night. She's been fortunate to publish a paranormal romance, *Twin Flames*, a paranormal romantic suspense, *Solstice* and a novella, *Forever Flames*, with Black Opal Books. She's had three short dark fiction stories published in anthologies and a paranormal holiday story in *Things That Go Bump For The Holidays*. Debbie is a member of RWA, her local chapter of RWA, and The International Thriller Writers, Inc. She lives in Connecticut with her husband and three children.